THE BIRD BOOK

Written by LAURA STORMS
Illustrated by SHARON LERNER

LERNER PUBLICATIONS COMPANY
MINNEAPOLIS, MINNESOTA

A NOTE ABOUT THE ART IN THIS BOOK

For the illustrations in this book, Sharon Lerner used a unique collage-like method. By arranging hundreds of paper scraps in overlapping patterns and using ink and watercolor for accent, she achieved special effects with color and texture for each bird.

For Sharon Lerner
—L.S.

For Leah Lerner
—S.L.

AN EARLY NATURE PICTURE BOOK

Library Of Congress Cataloging In Publication Data

Storms, Laura.
　　The bird book.

　　(An Early nature picture book)
　　Summary: Describes the habits, songs, and appearance of twelve North American birds including the robin, chickadee, and blue jay.
　　1. Birds—North America—Juvenile literature.
[1. Birds] I. Lerner, Sharon, ill. II. Title.
III. Series.
QL681.S76　　　　598.2973　　　　82-15189
ISBN 0-8225-1116-9　　　　　　AACR2

Manufactured in the United States of America

2　3　4　5　6　7　8　9　10　91　90　89　88　87　86　85　84　83

CONTENTS

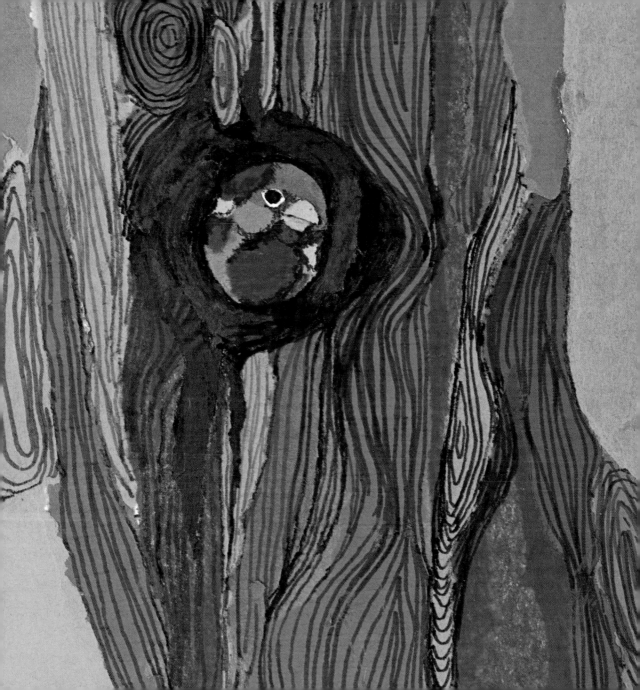

In the skies and in the treetops live many kinds of birds. Their busy habits, bright colors, and cheerful songs make birds a very special part of nature.

Many birds can be seen all through the year. But some birds disappear in the winter. They **migrate** (MY-grate), or fly to a warmer place, where they can find food more easily.

There are many, many kinds of birds. They are fun to watch. If you watch birds carefully, you can learn their colors, their songs, and their habits. Then you will be able to name some of the birds that you see in your yard or in the woods.

ROBIN

A sure sign of spring is the sound of a robin singing in the morning or early evening. Many people think the song sounds like "Cheer up, cheerily!" Usually the male robin sings this lovely song. He often sings as the eggs being watched by his mate are about to hatch.

Robins' nests are cup shaped and are found in trees or even on windowsills. Twice each spring, female robins lay two to four eggs. When these bright blue eggs hatch, both the male and the female help feed the baby robins.

Adult robins are experts at catching worms. The robin hops on the grass, stops, and cocks its head to see the ground better. Then it grabs the worm in its bill. The robin then flies quickly to its nest to feed the hungry babies waiting there.

BLUE JAY

It is very hard **not** to notice a blue jay! This large, noisy bird can be seen year-round in the deep woods or in your own backyard. Its bluish feathers are beautiful and bright. Another way to recognize a blue jay is by the **crest** on top of its head. A crest is a small tuft of feathers that looks like a pointed hat.

Blue jays are colorful birds. But many people do not like them. They have a loud, harsh cry, and they often chase smaller birds away. Blue jays are not all bad, though. They eat insects that can harm crops. And they often bury acorns and other seeds. By doing this, they help to plant trees for people to enjoy in years to come.

CARDINAL

One of the loveliest of all birds to see at any time of year is the cardinal. The cardinal is another bird that has a crest on its head. The male cardinal is completely red except for a small patch of black near his bill. Like many birds, the male is more colorful than the female. She is brownish with only a little red in her feathers. But the female is easy to spot, too. You can tell she's a cardinal from her bright orange-red bill and from the crest on her head.

Both male and female cardinals sing a loud, clear song. It sounds like "Sweet! Sweet! Sweet! **What** cheer! **What** cheer! **What** cheer!" Most birds sing only in spring and summer. But cardinals can be heard singing year-round.

CHICKADEE

Some birds are named for the sounds they make. The chickadee is one of these birds. It calls "Chick-a-dee-dee-dee!" in a buzzy voice. In the spring, male chickadees have another song, too. They whistle, "Fee-bee!" The first note is higher than the second.

Chickadees are friendly and tame. If you whistle at one, it may come closer to you. It might even eat right out of your hand. Chickadees can be seen all year. In winter, they like to eat from bird feeders.

Chickadees have a special talent. They can hang upside down from tree branches!

13

ROSE-BREASTED GROSBEAK

The male rose-breasted grosbeak is a very beautiful bird. His feathers are shiny black and snow white, and on his breast is a bright "bib" of rosy red. But like the cardinal, the male is much prettier than the female. She is plain and brown. These birds are excellent singers. Their song is cheerful and sounds much like a robin's.

Rose-breasted grosbeaks often build their nests in low branches. There the female lays four or five spotted eggs. It is fun to watch a nest and wait for the eggs to hatch. But never get too close! This will upset the mother and may cause her to leave the nest.

GOLDFINCH

The goldfinch is a pretty yellow bird. In the summer, the male's feathers are brighter than the female's. But in the winter, the male and female look very much alike.

Goldfinches like to stay together. Often they remain in flocks until mid- or late summer. Then, when they are sure to find plenty of food, they pair up and build nests. After the female lays her eggs, she almost never leaves the nest. While she keeps the eggs warm, the male brings her seeds to eat. Thistle seeds are one of her favorite foods.

Goldfinches soar in an up-and-down motion. As they fly, they sing "Per-chick-o-ree!" Sometimes it sounds like "Potato chips! Potato chips!"

RED-WINGED BLACKBIRD

Like the robin, the red-winged blackbird is a sign of spring. The male red-winged blackbird has very bright red patches on his shoulders. He fluffs up these red feathers to frighten enemies. Sometimes the red feathers do not show. Then only a pale yellow patch is seen.

Red-winged blackbirds gather in large numbers. They live near tall grasses, marshy ground, or in meadows. You may hear a red-winged blackbird singing his "O-ka-lee!" song near some cattails, where the female often builds her nest.

BALTIMORE ORIOLE

The male Baltimore oriole is a very brightly colored bird. His head is pure black, and his body is a brilliant orange. The female is pretty, too. She is yellow-green and has two white bars on each wing.

The nests of Baltimore orioles are very interesting. They are made of bark and parts of plants. Sometimes bits of yarn or string are used, too. The nest is shaped like a basket and holds four to six gray eggs. The nest is built so that the eggs cannot fall out easily, even in a strong wind.

The song of the Baltimore oriole is very lovely. In late spring, you can often hear baby Baltimore orioles as they whistle one or two loud, clear notes from their nests.

SONG SPARROW

There are many different kinds of sparrows. It is hard to tell these small birds apart without a lot of practice. But the song sparrow can be seen easily almost anywhere in the United States.

Look for the song sparrow perched near a river, pond, or lake. On warm spring or summer days, the males sing a cheerful song. They seem to love the beauty of the season. Their song sounds like "Hip-hip-hooray, boys! Spring is here!" But each bird's song is slightly different and has an important purpose. It is a signal used to mark each bird's **territory**, or the area where it will live and nest.

23

RED-HEADED WOODPECKER

Have you ever woken early in the morning to a loud tapping sound? Try to discover where the sound is coming from. Perhaps you will spot a red-headed woodpecker.

Woodpeckers use their stiff tail feathers to scoot up tree trunks. They hammer their long bills into the tree trunk where they find many insects to eat. Sometimes woodpeckers catch insects in midair. They swoop low and catch the insect with their bills.

There are many kinds of woodpeckers. Most of them have some red on their heads. But the red-headed woodpecker's head is **completely** bright red.

sharon Lerner

CEDAR WAXWING

Cedar waxwings are sleek brownish birds. They have a black "mask" around their eyes and a tufted crest on their heads. Cedar waxwings get their name from the hard, red, wax-like substance found on the tips of their wing feathers.

Cedar waxwings are nearly always found in flocks. They make a thin, buzzing "Zeee! Zeee!" sound as they fly from branch to branch looking for berries to eat. Often these birds will pass food along from one bird to the next until one waxwing finally eats it.

RUBY-THROATED HUMMINGBIRD

The hummingbird gets its name from the sound it makes. Its short wings flap so quickly that they make a humming, buzzing noise like a large flying insect. The hummingbird, our smallest bird, is only about 3½ inches long. Hummingbirds have shiny feathers, and their bright colors flash in the sunshine. In fact, you can only see the male's bright red throat when the sunlight hits it in a certain way. Hummingbirds are often called "flying jewels."

Hummingbirds fly nonstop from flower to flower. They use their long, thin bills like straws to suck nectar from the blossoms. These birds have such strong wings that they can fly backwards. They can even hover in the air like a helicopter!

THE BIRDS AROUND YOU

The next time you go outside, stop and listen carefully. Can you hear a bird singing? Watch closely when you see a bird moving in the branches of a tree. Notice the bird's color and shape. Maybe you will remember it as being one of the birds you saw in this book.

It is fun to learn about birds and to be able to name them. Birds are interesting. But most of all, they are wonderful to see and hear. Take the time to notice our bird friends. Without them, the morning skies would be silent, and the trees would be still. Birds are a beautiful part of nature all year long.

ABOUT THE AUTHOR

Laura Storms learned to love birds while spending summers in northern Michigan. There her older sister taught her that the rufous-sided towhee sings "Drink your tea!" and the white-throated sparrow sings "Poor Sam Peabody." She is now an avid birdwatcher and enjoys looking and listening for birds while walking in the woods, on the beach, or in her own backyard. Ms. Storms graduated from Lawrence University in Appleton, Wisconsin, where she studied music and education. She now works as an editor for a book publisher in Minneapolis.

ABOUT THE ARTIST

The published works of Sharon Lerner (1938-1982) combine her love of nature, art, and writing. As an artist, Ms. Lerner was recognized for her watercolors, collages, and jewelry. She earned a degree in art education from the University of Minnesota, was a lecturer and guide at the Walker Art Center and the Minneapolis Institute of Arts, and taught at University High School, Walker Art Center, and in the White Bear Lake (Minnesota) Public School system. During her 20-year career, Ms. Lerner wrote and illustrated 19 children's books, including *Places of Musical Fame*, *The Self-Portrait in Art*, *I Found a Leaf*, *The Flower Book*, *Who Will Wake Up Spring?*, *Orange Is a Color*, and *Butterflies are Beautiful*. Sharon Lerner lived in Minneapolis with her husband and four children. This is the last book she illustrated.